QABAR

QABAR

K.R. MEERA

Translated from the Malayalam
by Nisha Susan

eka

eka

First published in Malayalam as *Qabar* in 2000 by DC Books

Published in English as *Qabar* in 2021 by Eka, an imprint of Westland Publications Private Limited

1st Floor, A Block, East Wing, Plot No. 40, SP Infocity, Dr MGR Salai, Perungudi, Kandanchavadi, Chennai 600096

Westland, the Westland logo, Eka and the Eka logo are the trademarks of Westland Publications Private Limited, or its affiliates.

ISBN: 9789391234515

10 9 8 7 6 5 4 3 2 1

Typeset by SÜRYA, New Delhi

Printed at Thomson Press (India) Ltd.

ONE

The demolition of his ancestor's qabar—that was what his civil suit was about. I had read the whole thing the previous day and framed the issues. There was nothing wrong then. Everything was fine even at roll call. It was when I took up the case for cross-examination that everything fell apart. As soon as the name was called, I felt like I had been stabbed in the eye. I writhed in pain. Everything went dark for a bit. I was delirious. It was like nothing I had ever felt before. I forgot that I was the additional district judge and that I was in a courtroom. Yogishwaran Ammavan alone loomed large in my mind.

Yogishwaran Ammavan was an ancestor of ours. Legend had it that no head of the family had ever died at home until he did. As soon as they felt old, the uncles handed over the reins of all the family holdings to their heirs. Then they left for Kashi. No one who went to Kashi ever came back. Either they died on the way. Or they got to Kashi and lived there till they died and then dissolved in the Ganga. They got moksha even if they died en route. So, we never did the death rituals for those who went to Kashi. Only one man ever came back from Kashi. And that was Yogishwaran Ammavan.

One fine morning, the eldest nephew looked out into the yard and there he was, the ammavan whom he had sent off to Kashi with wails and tears. Five years later, standing in his front yard, healthier than ever, more glorious than ever. He was accompanied by two people. Two young girls. Outsiders. Sublime beauties.

This was a story I'd heard when I was a child. I had promptly forgotten it. But the memory surged up like someone rising from a grave. It stood right in front of me. Stood before me with matted hair that swept the floor, a beard that grazed his knees and stared at me. I was shaken. I had no time to hang about remembering old wives' tales. Every minute was precious. I had to hear nearly twenty cases back to back. On top of that, it was Progress Report Day at Advaith's school. I had requested the last appointment, at 5.30 p.m. If I got out at five, I'd be there on time. Advaith was a problem child and it was also important to have discussions with the psychologist at regular intervals. That's why I had started the afternoon session at 1.30 p.m.

That's when the fragrance reached me. It was a familiar perfume, a pleasant one. You know the Edward rose? That was the scent. Slowly, it became harsh. At first, I felt dizzy. And then I lost my mind. Like a string of pearls breaking, my concentration scattered and rolled away in every direction. I just about managed to finish the first case in the afternoon session. The second and third were appeals. The arguments ran longer than expected for the second case. In the third case, the defendant's lawyer began his arguments. But just five minutes in, he asked for it to be adjourned to the next day. And there we were, on the last case of the day. At 4 p.m., as I had hoped. I felt a little lighter.

The last case of the day. To be precise, OS/2/2019. Plaintiff: Kaakkasseri Khayaluddin Thangal; Defendant: Salahuddin Thangal and Others.

It was the plaintiff's cross-examination. During the clamour of roll call, I hadn't seen him. So, when the case was announced, I was expecting a skullcap, a mundu draped leftwards, a belt, a beard, no moustache, a clichéd Mappila. Right away, everything, including that assumption—went haywire. The man who climbed into the witness box was a hottie. I don't know why, but I lost my focus. I suddenly remembered going to see my mother to tell her that I had been appointed the additional district court judge. My mother was busy. She was dressing the wounds of a dog who had been hacked in the head and had lost some brain matter. The doctor was trying to unwind older bandages. The dog heaved and struggled. My mother held it along its belly, helped it stand straight, put her face against its ear and cuddled it. I held up the appointment order so my mother could read it. My mother's face brightened and her eyes welled up. But, the only thing she said was: 'Don't forget what EMS said.'

'What did EMS say?' Dr Sudhir asked as he unwound the sticky bandages. The dog was in pain. It wailed like a baby. My mother scratched its belly, comforted it and quoted from her memory without a pause or a stumble.

'Where the evidence is balanced between a well-dressed, pot-bellied rich man and a poor, ill-dressed and illiterate person, the judge instinctively favours the former.'

That was four years ago. When I sat in the judge's seat, it was the question I asked myself: was I going to habitually favour the pot-bellied tycoon or the pauper? Since then, I had thought often about the relationship between clothes and justice. One thing had become clear to me in the last four years. Those who were denied justice cared less about their appearance. Their clothes were likely to be soiled and their faces, sweaty. Not so for the one who has snatched someone else's money or happiness. He dresses well. He likes to adorn himself. Clothes are a sleight of hand—a handy trick to conceal the inner self and draw the eye to your outer self.

Kaakkasseri Khayaluddin Thangal had a good eye for clothes. A Fabindia linen silk Nehru jacket. Orange silk kurta. Sean Connery's body. Kamal Haasan's eyes. An unusual degree of self-confidence. The fragrance had become much sharper and its source had now become apparent. Our eyes met. I could see that his eyes were unusually brilliant. I looked again. They seemed to be gleaming, like two diamonds. They lit up his long eyelashes hypnotically. I tried to look away. I failed. His eyes became prisms. They turned the twilight into countless rainbows. My head hurt. Somehow, I managed to blink and look away. Instead of looking at him, I looked at his expensive lawyer. His face was obscured by the duelling rainbows. I shifted my gaze to the defendant's lawyer. His entire head was a rainbow.

I tried to read the document in my hands. Rainbows were scattered on the dark-green woollen tablecloth, like Advaith's multi-reference objects. I opened and closed my eyes. I shook my head. No improvement. Rainbows everywhere. The typist, the clerk, the typewriter, the calling bell and the peon were all rainbows. I looked behind me. Even Gandhiji in the portrait on the wall behind me had rainbows in place of his spectacle frames.

Those seven colours attacked my eyes like an army of seven thousand. My blood pressure soared. My skull cracked, brain exploded and eyes popped out of their sockets. The walls of the courtroom crumbled and I levitated. The table draped with the dark-green tablecloth on which was displayed the nameplate of 'Bhavana Sachidanandan Additional District Judge', a paperweight that said 'Work Is Worship' above neatly stacked files, a pen holder with Advaith's face printed on it, that familiar table and the chair, they both flew up to the sky. Someone placed a korandi palaka, an old-fashioned wooden seat, on the table and draped it with a zari-embroidered neriyathu. Yogishwaran Ammavan stood on the korandi palaka. I could see his feet clearly. They were worn out from walking. His soles were cracked and stamped with the maps of all the continents. On either side were the feet of the two girls. Their feet did not touch the korandi palaka. Their feet were not dirty. Those feet had walked on air. Two pairs of feet like freshly bloomed Edward roses, like newborn twins. I wanted to touch them. I stretched out my arms.

When my eyes opened, I was in hospital. Light dawned gradually and my memory seemed reluctant to return. It took a couple of minutes for the system to boot and then every connection came alive with a scream. I panicked: 'My child', 'his school', 'PTA', 'progress report'. I was stricken with anxiety that Advaith was still waiting for me in school. A child with ADHD. A child who, sometimes, no one else could manage. I shook like a leaf. As soon as I caught sight of my bag on the table, I picked it up and ran out. The tube in the cannula dragged and the IV drip stand toppled over. The cannula popped out of my arm, spraying blood. My steno Roshi and office assistant Selina ran towards me. Nurses raced up, straightened the stand and stuck a Band-aid on my arm. Selina held me close. I forgot that I was a district judge, leant my head on her shoulder and sobbed for Advaith. 'My baby, my baby.'

'Don't worry, madam. Roshi picked up your son and dropped him home.' Selina wiped my eyes with her dupatta.

'Is Manju at home? Or has she left?'

'Manju isn't going home today. Everything is fine at home.'

'I've inconvenienced all of you, haven't I?'

'What inconvenience? As long as you're okay, madam.'

'I don't know what happened. It was very sudden. I felt like I had floated up to the sky.'

'All we saw was you slumping forward on the table.'

'Has it been long since you brought me here?'

'Two and a half hours, that's all.'

'And I was unconscious the whole time?'

'The case was announced exactly at 4 p.m. Madam, you slumped forward less than two seconds later. We reached the hospital in ten minutes. When we saw the doctor, it was exactly 4.15.'

I sat at the head of the bed, leaning on my elbow. That's when Dr Smitha Rani walked in.

'All well, madam?' she asked.

'I think so.' I tried to smile.

'You don't just think so. Everything is okay. Everything is normal.'

'Then what happened to me?'

'When you came in, your BP was very low. Tomorrow and the day after are both holidays, right? Rest well. Watch a comedy or listen to music and de-stress.'

'When can I go home?'

'As soon as possible. We don't want any healthy people here.'

Everyone laughed. But I couldn't laugh. Something was lodged in my eye. A shard of that rainbow. Everywhere I looked, I saw its muted colours. That unworldly violet especially.

It took another hour to get to my quarters. Roshi drove us. Advaith was staging a satyagraha at our doorstep, still in his school uniform, with his bag still slung on his shoulders. As soon as I stepped out of the car, leaning on Selina's shoulder, he ran up to me and shook me. He hit me on my chest and head. 'Bad Amma', 'broke your promise', 'told lies', he wept. Then he saw the bandage on my arm. And then began the frantic hugging, the wailing and the rolling on the ground. 'What has happened to my mother? Is my mother going to die? What will happen to me now?' he screamed. I managed to console him and get him inside the house. I made him change out of his uniform and gave him a bath. I had a quick bath as well and put on the first salwar-kurta I found in the cupboard.

Like a weighing scale with one empty bowl, I had no balance. I found it hard to stay upright. When I came out with my wet hair wrapped in a towel, Manju was serving cake and tea to Roshi and Selina. Once I fed Advaith, things were a bit calmer. Friday evenings, 6 to 8 p.m., was his movie time. The psychologist's instructions were to keep movies and video games to the absolute minimum. I couldn't stick to them entirely. After I put on a movie for him, I came back to the drawing room.

'What a strange day!' I tried to break the ice. 'It's the first time in my life that something like this has happened. I must be getting old,' I joked. Selina and Roshi exchanged glances.

'Madam, you probably won't believe it. But the reason this happened was that Thangal,' said Selina.

'Which one?' I asked.

'Kaakkasseri Thangal. The plaintiff in today's cross-examination. He comes from a line of djinn-worshippers,' Roshi said with great hesitation.

I wanted to laugh.

'Isn't he an architect, Roshi? And he is well educated.'

Roshi continued, 'I overheard the lawyers talking about it. You know Shyam Krishnan saar. He is this Thangal's lawyer. His daughter lives in Bangalore. They found out today at noon that she has had a baby. She is his only daughter. He checked and found that there was a 7.30 p.m. flight to Bangalore. But to get on that flight, he would have to leave the court at least at 4 p.m. When Thangal heard the news, he apparently assured the lawyer—go ahead and buy the ticket, the judge won't sit in court for a second longer than 4 p.m.'

'That must be why he doused himself in that perfume. As soon as I smelt it, my head started hurting,' I scoffed.

'Not that, madam. At the lawyer's office, in front of all the juniors, that man took Shyam Krishnan's hand and swore, "If the judge sits in her chair for more than two seconds after 4 p.m. ..."'

'If I did ...?'

'Then he would unleash someone called Yogishwaran.'

Selina had said this casually, but my smile faded. Fear crawled inside my heart like a reptile with thorny spines on its underbelly instead of scales. Roshi and Selina continued talking, but I heard none of it. I must have said something about feeling sleepy because they left soon after. I lay on my bed. I was drenched in sweat. An unfamiliar figure loomed in front of me. Seven or eight feet tall. Broad chest. A great cloud of long, matted hair that had grown over centuries. A grey moustache that hung to his belly. Grey ash marks on his forehead and in the middle, a trishul drawn in blood. Long, long nails. Deep cracks on the soles of his feet. Toenails twisted like a banyan's overhanging roots.

The reptile was now coiled around my heart. Advaith came to bed. I hugged him and tried to forget my terror. 'Why is your heart making these loud theem-theem sounds,' he asked. One shouldn't lie to children. So I told him, 'Amma is feeling scared.' I choked a little as I said it. My poor baby. He reassured me, 'Don't worry, Amma, you've got me.' He was all I had. I held him tighter. He fell asleep right away.

The judge in the court of sleep rejected my petition. I tossed and turned. I felt like Yogishwaran Ammavan was in my bedroom. I tried to forget him. Instead,

I examined the memory of levitating. An experience I had never had before. An experience I had never even imagined. Sitting on a chair in the sky. Leaning my elbows on the desk and peering down. Below, the civil station, the town and the hills. To the right, fields, churches, apartments. On the left, a temple, the stadium, the bridge, the bypass. And right below that chair in the sky, the collectorate where my mother had worked as a peon. Prohibition activists on relay protests, who didn't know there was a woman up in the sky. People wandering inside and outside the collectorate.

I felt my tension ease. I remembered a sky filled with clouds. Clouds like the bearded, white seeds of milkweed. They brushed against my cheeks, eyes and neck. Whether it was a djinn or a demon, it had been an extraordinary experience. I felt grateful to have had an encounter with someone who could make rainbows bloom with his eyes. I worked hard not to float up towards the ceiling with its cracks and fading paint. From mid-air, I surveyed the bed with its pink-roses-on-white sheets, the nine-year-old boy sleeping on his belly and my body that hugged him. I felt pity and contempt for this body that had been embraced only by its own child for six whole years.

I landed back with a thump. My outer self had become a qabar. Its dark depth took in my inner self.

I thought of Thangal who had raised Yogishwaran Ammavan from the dead to defeat me, and I writhed. I felt violent. 'You may be a judge, but you are still a woman, aren't you? Just a woman,' I heard his thoughts, full of scorn. My self-esteem was wounded. I swore I would show him that there are no men or women in court, only the goddess of justice. Him with his djinn and his Edward rose perfume and his linen silk jacket!

I went to the drawing room. Opening the box of case documents, I dug out the lawsuit.

OS/2/2019

Plaintiff
K. Khayaluddin Thangal
Kaakkasseril
Kottayam

Defendant
K. Salahuddin Thangal and 61 others

I'd read it before, but I read through again carefully. This was the gist.

K. Salahuddin Thangal, K. Fasaluddin Thangal, K. Ameeruddin Thangal, sons of K. Nisaruddin Thangal together sold two acres, fifteen cents of family property to the owner of the property adjacent to 'T' property, the Saketam Charitable Trust, at the rate of Rs 1.75 lakh per acre. The party that bought 'T' property had begun construction on the site. Due to these activities, an ancestral qabar and tombstones on the southern end of 'T' property had been demolished. Though the plaintiff was prepared to buy the land required to preserve the qabar, the trust was not ready to sell him the property. The suit asked for a speedy intervention to prevent the destruction of a site that was sacred to the plaintiff because it contained the relics of his ancestor, who had gone to Mecca back in the day.

I examined the issues that I had framed earlier.

1. Was it possible to conduct a valuation of the disputed property?
2. The property that was transferred had been given to a charitable trust for public use. Were all the documents of the transaction in order?
3. Did the claim have standing?
4. According to Islamic beliefs, was a qabar permitted on private property? Was any meezan stone installed to identify the qabar?

I examined the evidence. The documents that the plaintiff had submitted were letters unconnected to the case, personal letters. The sale deed submitted by the defendant and the plans for the proposed auditorium submitted by the Saketam Charitable Trust were all in order. I began to feel vengeful. I could already see the lines I'd write in the judgement, but I didn't write it. To write the judgement without a hearing—that's not justice. No need to wonder whether justice is male or female. Justice is a woman. A blindfolded woman.

I put aside the bundle and exhaled with relief. As I lay down, pressing my face against my son's bony back, I was afraid I'd dream of Yogishwaran Ammavan that night. It was time to issue a ruling to my mind: strictly no dreams about Yogishwaran Ammavan. Instead, I saw Kaakkasseri Khayaluddin Thangal, with Sean Connery's figure and Kamal Haasan's eyes. Rather than send Yogishwaran Ammavan, he had entered the stage himself. In his hands, he held a single pink Edward rose. With its big petals, he drew lines from my throat to my forehead to my eyes, and from my nose to my cheeks to my ears. He drew without drawing. I writhed, but he showed no mercy. I was exhausted by the tortuous tickling all night and jolted awake at six in the morning. No flowers on the bed. But at the tip of my nose was that floral aroma that had wafted through the courtroom. The Edward rose with the gentle fragrance that you never tire of.

[illegible] Western [illegible] world any [illegible]
[illegible] new, [illegible] Indian influence
[illegible] that's [illegible]
[illegible] hard to wonder whether she is male or
[illegible] a woman? A Hindooed woman.
[illegible] and exhaled [illegible]. As
[illegible] down [illegible] against [illegible] body
[illegible] Cesare [illegible]
[illegible] was [illegible]
[illegible] Yoshiwara [illegible] America.
[illegible] He [illegible]
[illegible] figure [illegible]
[illegible] Yoshiwara [illegible] America [illegible] he had
[illegible] hand [illegible] single
[illegible] eyes, and from
[illegible] with no
[illegible] I was
[illegible]
[illegible] the bed.
[illegible] aroma that
[illegible] The Pathfinder.
[illegible] that you never tire of.

TWO

The eldest nephew woke up one morning, washed his face and found the uncle who had gone to Kashi standing in the front yard. He screamed in shock. The liegemen came running. They absorbed the fact of the ammavan's return with a sense of disbelief. Someone brought a long-nosed kindi of water. A korandi was produced and then a clean neriyathu. They made him stand on the korandi and washed his feet. Yogishwaran Ammavan stretched his arms out to both sides. Then the two girls hopped on to the korandi. Men in that household were not in the habit of washing young girls' feet. But the eldest nephew didn't have the guts to disobey Yogishwaran Ammavan's orders. The girls' clothes were made of Kashi silk and heavily pleated. What they wore, it wasn't a skirt. Nor was it a dress. The older one stood on the korandi. She lifted the hem of her garment, with its gold threads and many pearls. The eldest nephew, who was old enough to be her father, bent before her resentfully. When he was about to pour the water from the kindi, he realised her feet weren't touching the ground. His eyes nearly popped. Then the younger one raised her skirts. She was standing on air too. The nephew's head spun. He toppled backwards, kindi, water and all.

All this, my father narrated as if he had been right there when it happened. I had gone to my father's house on Saturday, hoping to hear this story, having wheedled Advaith into coming with me. 'Please rest, madam. Don't drive,' Selina and Manju had pleaded. But I didn't listen to them. When I heard the overwrought background music all the way from the gate, I realised my plans were going to flop. Who knew there were TV serials on Saturday too? When I reached the veranda, I heard dialogue at an ear-splitting volume.

'How did it turn out, dear?'

'Since Mother confessed, the court remanded her.'

It went on. The background music, the emotional drama, the suspense. I stood at the doorway holding Advaith's hand. My father was sitting in the planter's chair, leaning eagerly towards the TV with the remote clutched in one hand. His face was resting on his knee, and his knee on the long arm of the chair.

The young man on screen was saying things like,

'For Mother, being in jail is as good as being dead. But she confessed to her crime.'

Fed up, I called out loudly, 'Acha!' Achan didn't turn to look. Instead, he moved the remote from his left hand to his right to hold it more securely. Then he raised his left hand to gesture, 'Wait'. Luckily, an ad came on. My father's body relaxed a little. He leant back with a deep sigh and ventured a pleasantry. 'Oh, it's you, is it?'

When he saw Advaith, he tucked the remote even more securely into his armpit and exhibited common courtesy by saying, 'Come here, sweetie, come and tell me how you are.'

'When it was telecast yesterday, I couldn't watch it,' he explained without being asked. But his eyes were on the screen, alert for the end of the ad. 'Bharat, Meena and the kids have gone to Meena's folks because it's a bank holiday,' he said, again without my asking. Subtext being, there was no need for me to hang around too long, waiting to see them. Wasting no time, I gave Advaith the bag with the Ensure, D-Protin and oats to hand over to his grandfather. As Advaith approached, my father screwed the remote even tighter into his armpit, making me laugh.

'Alright then, I'll come back when there is no serial on.'

I turned to go. Right then, with a loud 'theem', the

electricity went. The television and my father both went off.

'Unbearable! Them and their transformer repairs!' he cursed and called my brother a bastard for not hooking up the TV to the invertor. And then, without a pause, he said, 'Why don't you stay then,' suddenly all affection. It would last only until the electricity came back. To get to my goal, I made small talk. 'Your blood tests were normal, weren't they?'

It was as if he was waiting for me to ask. 'Tests! What is the point of getting tests done in my old age and becoming a burden on everyone? No more tests. No more drugs. I am seventy years old. If I take to my bed, who will help me get to the loo?' he grumbled.

'You have a wife and children, don't you?' I said innocently.

My father was incensed. 'Wife? What wife? That woman who walked out on her elderly husband, is she a wife?'

I hid my laughter.

'Amma brought home a dog whose leg was crushed by a car. You flipped out. Amma begged you to put up with the dog just until its leg healed. You were adamant. You said, either me or the dog. Amma decided that she only wanted the dog. How is that a crime?'

'I mean less than a street dog, that's the meaning of

what she did, isn't it? What happened to my standing in the world? Your brother's? Yours? Our clan's? She was just an employee in the lowest grade. At least I was a Lower Division Clerk. Given our family status, I could have said, stay at home, I don't want my wife to do lowest-grade work. I could have. Did I say it? No. Why? Because I didn't want my wife to starve if I died. I was being considerate. Was she ever grateful?'

'Didn't you tell me it was because you couldn't live on one salary?'

'So, because you are a judge now, you don't need to show respect to your father?'

My father sulked. I became serious.

'When you married Amma and brought her home, she was twenty years old. It was two kilometres to your village office. It took Amma two hours to get to her Collectorate office. Amma woke up at 3 a.m. every day to make breakfast, lunch and snacks for you, for us kids, for Appoopan and Ammooma, and then ran full tilt for the 8 a.m. bus. She used to pleat her sari while running for the bus. She rushed back into the house at seven in the evening. She'd change out of her sari and go straight into the kitchen. Fish curry, two different vegetables, prep for the next morning's breakfast. Until she retired at fifty-six, I never saw my mother sit down once, not even on a Sunday.'

'Every woman in this country does all that. Does

that mean you leave your husband in your old age and shame him like a dog in front of everyone?'

'Whose fault is it if Amma feels that the dog whose wound she treated yesterday is more loving than you who doesn't remember everything she did for thirty-six whole years?'

My father looked shocked. Then he fell silent. I soothed him.

'Acha, I didn't come to pick a fight. I came to ask you about something. Have you heard of the Kaakkasseri Thangals?'

'Traditionally they are doctors and sorcerers. Don't know what they are like now.'

'Isn't the occult haraam for Muslims?'

'It's not our kind of sorcery, with fire and herbs. It's djinn worship. Haven't you heard of Kaakkasseri Bhattathiri? He was a great scholar. And you know the Bhattathiris are elites even among the Brahmins. But as time went by, he gave up on notions of purity and pollution and poojas. The Brahmins got together and did a pooja to "fix" him. He left town. No word of him after that. The story goes that when he was hounded out of his town, he came here and lived incognito, and that when he died, the king gave his house to the Jonakans—the Turks who had come for trade. And that is how the Thangals supposedly got the Kaakkasseri family name. And that is how the

Thangals supposedly got the Kaakkasseri family name. The other story is that they got it because people called Muslims "Kaakkas". Who knows if it is true? It's all myth and legend.'

'What kind of sorcery did they do?'

My father paused and looked at the TV, eyes filled with the sweet sorrow of parting. Then he continued: 'They'd exorcise the possessed. They can chant to remove obstacles from your path. But … when did you start believing in this stuff?'

I didn't have to reply. With another loud 'theem', the electricity came back on. The overwrought BGM started again. A thousand neon lights illuminated my father's face. I felt a maternal affection for him. Leaving him to his emotionally charged drama, I stepped out. I walked towards our old family home. It was a small house with four rooms. Till twelve years ago, that was where we had lived. When Amma first came here, it had a thatched roof. Later, it got a tiled one. When Achan received his inheritance, he bought out his sisters' share of the house.

I sat on the steps of the old house, in front of its locked front door. When I was about to get married, I had wept and wailed and gone on a hunger strike. That's how the new concrete house next door was built. But my father didn't tear down this old house. It was a piece of history. I sat there. I looked east. In the north-eastern direction, I saw dark clouds. In the heart of those clouds was a rainbow. Was it someone's spell? I blinked. Thirteen hundred years ago, did rainbows look like this? What did this land look like back then? What trees and plants grew here? What did human beings think, do, wear back then? That was the only way to properly understand Yogishwaran Ammavan. In his time, the house was a sprawling pathinaru kettu with sixteen halls and four courtyards. The story goes that the family had a falling out with the king, and he deployed that classic punishment of razing their house and having a pond dug in its place. In another version, the house was destroyed because of the family's wasteful, extravagant ways. Anyway, it was thrilling to imagine that Yogishwaran Ammavan had brought those two girls to where I was sitting. I got goosebumps.

'It's gone again.' My father had come in search of me, sighing in despair. He dusted the veranda with his hand and sat down.

'Acha, wasn't there a Yogishwaran Ammavan here?' I asked.

My father rolled his eyes at me.

'What do you mean, *was*? He is still here. He is the one who keeps this family safe.'

Achan began telling the story. It was a story I knew, but it was fun to sit there listening. Yogishwaran

Ammavan hoisted the girls whose feet didn't touch the ground on his shoulders and took them inside the house. In the east room, the one with the thatched roof and cowdung-tempered floor, where honoured guests were received, he set the children on korandis in the auspicious south-western corner. He lit a lamp respectfully. Asked them what they wanted to eat. The children asked for food untouched by fire or rain. Yogishwaran Ammavan went to fetch them tender coconut water. When he came back with the coconut water, the korandis in the eastern room lay empty. He was worried. Elder One, Younger One, he called out to them loudly. Inside the sacred grove where the beeches, the black varnish trees, the bahedas and the paper flower vines made it pitch dark even at high noon, the Elder One heard his call. The Younger One, swinging on the vine of a creeping treebine, fully fifty leagues long and suspended between a teak and a rosewood so tall that it scraped the sky, also heard his call.

Unfortunately for me, just as my father had reached this point of the story, the electricity came back. My father sped inside. I was left alone. Then Advaith, who had been sitting inside the new house all this time, meandered up to me. 'Why are you sitting here?' he asked harshly. His face was sullen. I quailed a little.

'This is your grandfather's ancestral home,' I said

cautiously. He stuck his finger in his nose and looked around. My heart began to sink.

In English he asked, 'So Appoopan was also deserted by his dad?'

That came out of nowhere. My nerves flagged. I couldn't think of a reply. I rose and went up to him. I held him and patted his hair. Kissed both his cheeks two or three times. He looked at me like a judge. Then he shoved me aside in disgust. The next phase would involve physical violence. Clawing and scratching. Sometimes biting. I felt my courage and confidence drain away. It was best to leave right away. I didn't dawdle. I went inside and said goodbye to my father. He had returned to the position we had found him in. Now he raised his left hand at us. Tightened his grip on the remote control.

As the car reached the main road, Advaith was simmering. He lay down in the backseat. Then knelt on the seat. Tried to roll down the windows. Drank water. Poured some on his clothes. Threw the bottle down, spilling water on the floor of the car. Crushed the biscuits in the seat pocket and mixed it with the water to make a thick paste.

'Advaith ...' I called out softly, looking at him in the rearview mirror. He shook his head defiantly.

'Which movie does my baby want to watch today?'

First there was silence. Then a scream.

'I don't want to watch any movie!'

My heart raced. I tried to drive as fast as possible. From the backseat, he shoved his head forward until it was next to mine, gnashed his teeth and yelled, 'Did Appoopan have ADHD?'

I was startled. Any answer could be dangerous. With a trembling heart, I waited for an imminent explosion. Checked again that the child lock was on. I stopped the car on the side of the road. He hit me hard on my shoulder. Face contorted, he asked, 'If he didn't, then why did Appoopan's father abandon him?'

'Appooppan's father died. He didn't desert him,' I said with great care.

'But my father abandoned me, didn't he?'

He shook me hard. I didn't react. I turned towards the back seat and looked him in the eye.

'Advaith, I have told you before, haven't I, that your father didn't leave us because of your ADHD?'

'Yes, he did. Yes, yes, yes, yes!'

He pushed me aside like he was possessed by a poltergeist and then fell backwards in the seat and rolled and thrashed. I felt ready to collapse. My tears were choking me, but there was no way I could cry.

'Sweetie ...' I called again.

I said, this time in English, 'I have told you a thousand times, haven't I? We didn't separate because of you. I have told you, haven't I? Your father didn't like that I had become a judge. That is why we split.'

He replied in English too. 'You are lying! You are a liar! You are a cheat! You are a devil!'

Eyes rolling, teeth gnashing, he jumped up and down in the car. He thrashed around on the seat and on the floor of the car and wept. I closed my eyes and counted silently. One, two, three. When I reached seventy-five, the sobbing in the backseat had subsided. I started driving again. Unfortunately, it started raining just then. Big, pouring rain. The rest of the drive was hellish. Endless traffic, the sky's tears, my tears. It was after seven when we reached the quarters. Selina had released Manju from duty and taken her place. She said that Kunjumol, who came to clean and cook, had left already.

As soon as I realised I was going to be a single parent for the rest of my life, I had written the exam for District Judge selection. I had one reason and one reason only. As a judge, I'd be allotted two office assistants. I'd have one by my side all the time.

I found it hard to scoop up Advaith, who was asleep in the backseat. He had grown, my baby. As I carried him, asleep on my shoulder, I became those broken scales again. By the time I lay him down in bed, I was exhausted. I tucked him in and turned away, only to have him clutch my hand. My heart stopped. I braced myself for another explosion. But he was calm.

'Amma, don't tell lies,' he said in English.

'Advaith, your Amma has never lied to you.'

I was upset and he melted. 'Then, why did Achan leave us?'

'No one left anyone. Achan and Amma separated.'

'It was because of me, wasn't it? Because I am differently abled?'

One must not lie to children. I looked him in the eye.

'No. Your ADHD isn't such a big deal. Fathers don't leave their babies when even bigger problems crop up. Especially a brilliant, smart, angel baby like you.'

His cheeks reddened.

'So, my father didn't leave because of me?'

'No. It's because Pramod has a personality disorder.'

'What's his problem?'

'Lack of empathy.'

'Is that a disorder?' He sat up, eager to know.

'That's the world's biggest disorder.'

'So, it's not because he doesn't love me?'

'He has no love in him because of his disorder.'

'So, his lack of love is not his fault ...'

'Not at all. It's just a condition.'

'So, we shouldn't be angry with Achan.'

'No ...'

He laughed. I leant over and ran my fingers through

his hair. My child had Pramod's brown eyes, thick eyebrows, and his long, prominent nose. When he grew up, Advaith was going to be the spitting image of his father. Pramod definitely had a narcissistic personality disorder. The day the doctor said Advaith might have ADHD, Pramod had screamed, 'I never again want to see this cursed little animal who never gives us a moment's peace.'

For a little while, I continued to kiss him. I tickled his ears. I asked my question with extreme care.

'Advaith, what made you think of your father today?'

'That ... that's because I saw your father.' He looked shifty.

'See, someone is telling a big lie,' I teased him.

His face was filled with guilt. He turned over and pressed his face into the pillow. Then turned back over.

'Amma, I saw a card on Appoopan's table.'

'What card?'

'A wedding card.'

I became numb. It was a moment I had expected.

'Advocate K. Rajagopal Araykkal and Indira Rajagopal cordially invite you to the wedding of their dear son Adv. Pramod Araykkal with Advocate Priyanka on 2 September 2019 at ...'

I didn't allow him to continue his recital. I lavished him with kisses on his cheeks and throat. 'We have escaped, haven't we?' I joked. I tickled him. He rolled about and laughed. Until he was bathed, fed and asleep, I made him laugh with all kinds of silliness.

As soon as I was sure he was asleep, I collapsed. I fought hard not to cry. But since the Indian Penal Code has no sections regulating crying and laughing, I failed. I regretted going to law college and not taking up sorcery and mesmerism instead.

Falling in love with Pramod in college. Fasting every Monday for six or seven years to become Pramod's wife. Making my father take a loan to build a concrete house so as not to shame Pramod when he eventually came home with his proposal and his wealthy relatives. Skimping and saving everything I earned while I was Kurup Sir's junior to buy 100 sovereigns of gold. Giving up big cases after we got married when I realised my winning them was creating a forest fire of insecurity in Pramod. Deciding not to write the Munsiff Magistrate selection test because Pramod had not passed it.

There was a woman who had done all these things. That woman never wore a sari that Pramod didn't like. She didn't speak to anyone Pramod didn't like. She found no joy in things unless they gave Pramod joy. She didn't want to breathe without asking Pramod for permission. If I had studied sorcery, I could have nailed her feet down and caned her from head to toe to exorcise her. I could have plucked her teeth and nails out and beheaded her on an altar. I could have issued orders to nail her remains on a yakshi pala tree for the next 7,000 years.

If I had studied magic as soon as Advaith showed signs of a meltdown, I could have picked him up and flown high in the sky, distracted him by plucking toffees out of the trees. Made the birds tell him stories when he was bored. Most importantly, if I had studied magic, I could have hypnotised everyone in the vicinity whenever I wanted to cry. I could have cried to my heart's content without anyone seeing me.

When I lay down, holding Advaith close, I seriously considered the possibility of studying sorcery and illusions. I wanted him as my guru—Kaakkasseri Khayaluddin Thangal. I am not sure when I fell asleep. But when I woke up, the room was filled with the dizzying smell of the flowers of the yakshi pala tree.

THREE

Kaakkasseri Bhattathiri got that name from his ability to tell one kaakka from another. He was assured in his ability to tell the crow he had seen the previous day from the crow he had seen the previous week. That was supposed to be a sign of his intelligence. I didn't believe that legend. To recognise human beings, you need to remember them. For us to recognise birds and beasts, they need to distinguish themselves by remembering us. That's not a function of intelligence. I was convinced of it when I went to see my mother on Sunday. My mother had more than thirty in her brood now. Several of them came running when they saw me. That's when I recognised them. 'Any time folks in the vicinity see a puppy, they bring them here,' said my mother happily.

Seeing the canine progeny's sincere affection towards my mother, I felt such a sense of inferiority.

She had carried me in her belly for nine months. She had suffered to bring me into the world. She had certainly suffered to keep me breastfed. Still, I didn't love my mother unconditionally the way these creatures did. 'This one, he is very short-tempered.' 'She is very possessive.' 'There he is, the purest manifestation of laziness.' 'Take a look at this one, if someone hurts him, all hell breaks loose.' 'A rich man bought this one for a lot of money. He was very loving towards her. But he also beat her very badly. One day, he crossed the line and hit her too much. She bit him and ripped him to shreds. He picked up his gun and shot her. That's why she has this broken gait.' My mother introduced each son and daughter this way.

When Advaith kissed his grandmother, most of the thirty-two progeny made a ruckus to be included. 'Me too! Me too!' I saw the one who had suffered that terrible wound four years ago pushing his way to the front with his misshapen head. When my mother said, 'After I am gone, you will look after them, won't you?' Advaith was over the moon.

We got a little time together, Amma and I, in the middle of all this horseplay and laughing and joking. That's when I said to her, 'The other day, I fainted in court.'

My mother was cuddling Sonu, who had broken his leg when a car hit him. Didn't say a word. To her children she said, 'Sonu, Meenu, Chakki, go to your cage. Jackie, you over here. Cookie, you over there. If you make trouble, you will all get it from me.' Having issued these orders, she rose. 'Come, let's go inside and talk,' she said to me. She untied her apron and hung it up on the hanger beside the veranda. Soaped and washed her hands. Dried them on a towel. Then went inside unhurriedly. I followed her.

This was a house made of mud. It had a hall, a kitchen and a bathroom. That was it. In this house, everything Amma wanted, she had at her fingertips. And it had nothing that Amma didn't want. When my mother married my father and went to live with him, she had a tin trunk. The trunk contained books and four sets of clothes. Over time, the trunk had corroded. And when my mother left my father's home, that's still pretty much all she had—a few changes of clothes and two cardboard boxes full of books. There was lots of space left even in the Maruti car I had back then.

I gave Advaith my phone to play games on and went into the kitchen. My mother was boiling water for our tea. On the shelf, alongside small baskets of onions and potatoes, was a small English book, facedown. I took a look. *The Vegetarian* by Han Kang. 'Meena bought that one for me. Good book,' she said. 'With this judge job of yours, you have no time to read novels, I suppose!' she added rudely.

'Why don't you come and spend a day with me, Amma? Then you will understand how easy and relaxing my job is.'

'Two hours to the office. Two hours back home. Sitting when I had a seat. Standing when I didn't have one. That's how I read all that I read.'

My mother was braced to argue. I joined my hands and bowed. She laughed and poured out the tea. Then I told her what had happened in court. As she handed me the cup, she looked sharply at me.

'Is it stress because of Pramod's wedding?'

'I heard about that. But no. That wasn't it.'

'I got a card too.'

'He might send me one too.'

I tried to smile, but it became a grimace.

'No. It's because it isn't right to send you one that they sent me and Achan cards to get the news to you.'

'A great man.'

'Some other stress?'

I swore to my mother that the day I'd fainted, all I had been stressed about was getting to my son's school at 5.30 p.m. My mother didn't believe me. Then I told her what Selina and Roshi had told me—Kaakkasseri Khayaluddin Thangal's threat.

Amma laughed. 'Telepathy and hypnosis are probably real. But no Yogishwaran or Thangal can barge into your mind unless you want them to.'

'I am a little scared, Amma.'

'I always thought judges have no capacity for feeling fear, distress or compassion for the poor,' my mother mocked me. A little later, she asked, 'Did you tell your father about this?'

'I didn't tell him about fainting in court. I asked about Thangal. Achan said that the Kaakkasseri people came from Jonakans. Are they Muslim sorcerers?'

'Mohammedan. Turks. Greeks. Those are the meanings of Jonakan, I think. At one point in time, Jonakan was the generic name for all the traders who came from other parts of the world. I think I remember a visiting speaker talking about it at a trade union convention. Also, in the northern districts, that's what they call those who converted to Islam during the time of Tipu Sultan's assaults.'

She drank the tea in her cup in two quick swallows and asked, 'Do you know why your father doesn't like dogs?'

'Isn't it because of the family taboo against keeping dogs?'

'When the nephews buried Yogishwaran Ammavan in the courtyard, it's a dog who scratched and clawed and dug him up.'

'What dog was that?'

'A dog that came with him from Kashi. Poor thing. It was showing gratitude for having been fed occasionally.'

I felt chilled.

'But Achan didn't mention a dog. Just the children who came with him.'

'He wouldn't, would he? Did he mention Ammavan being buried? I am guessing not.'

'The two children were goddesses. He sat them down beside him and attained nirvana. Isn't that the legend?'

'This is what happens when you have too much pride in your traditions. You can't talk about everything openly. Then you end up manufacturing a new legend.'

My mother laughed pitilessly. I was at a loss for words. It occurred to me that the plaintiff who had come to my court one afternoon, wafting a strange fragrance, was making my life rather complicated. I really wanted to see Kaakkasseri Thangal and sort out my confusions. But I feared it too. When I saw him next, whom would he push into my mind? Yogishwaran Ammavan? Or Kaakkasseri Bhattathiri? Or the great scholars whom Bhattathiri had defeated in debate? In any case, before I finished drinking the tea my mother gave me, I came to two decisions—one, to notify the case right away. Two, to conclude it in a week.

On the drive back, Advaith was happy. He chattered non-stop. When I stopped on the way to buy him pizza, he insisted on trying to make friends with the girl at the next table. He let them know that his grandmother had thirty-two children. In half an hour, he managed to break a glass and get everyone's attention by dropping two spoons.

It was dusk when we got home. Then there was a lot of rushing about. Advaith's homework-school-diary-book-sorting-feeding-bedtime. Some small chores of my own. When it was all done, I was suddenly alone. I could have spent some more time talking to my mother, I thought. My divorce and my mother's moving out had happened around the same time. Amma had retired in 2013. I had been married seven years then.

Two nights before my wedding, my mother had come into my room and lay down next to me in my bed. For the first time since I had become an adult. I hugged her joyfully. Put my head on her chest. My mother said in a quavering voice:

'Tradition has it that, after you are married, three-fourth of my duties as a mother will be finished.'

'Is a mother's duty the kind of thing that gets done,' I pouted.

'What do you mean? What else is left to be done? When you are about to have a child, I will come and help you for a while. Help you until the children are three or four years old.'

'And after that?'

'I will go to Kashi.'

I laughed. 'Sure! I can just see Achan coming along!'

'Alone.'

'I can just see Achan letting you go!'

'I am talking about ending this business of asking for permission.'

I didn't understand a thing. But my mother's voice was coming from the depths of her heart.

'I want a place of my own, Bhavana.'

'What are you saying, Amma?'

I sat up. Amma sat up too. She held my hand, looked into my eyes and said with great seriousness, 'I am retiring in seven years. By then I want a scrap of land and a one-room house. A room of my own.'

I sat there shell-shocked. My mother continued:

'When I am nearing home at seven o'clock at night, sometimes I am the only one in that back lane. My one companion on that stretch used to be a brown dog. I would feed him leftover teatime snacks from the office. One day, I saw that a car had hit him and broken his leg. He had tears streaming down his face. I couldn't just stand there and do nothing. I picked him up and brought him here. I did it because I thought this was my house.'

'Why are you talking like a child, Amma? Isn't this your house?'

'That's the day I understood that this isn't my house. I can't bring home a hapless animal if I want to. I have no right to give it a place to rest or feed it for a day if I want to.'

'What are you saying, Amma? Wasn't that because Achan hates all dogs?'

'Shall I demonstrate this by bringing home a human being tomorrow?'

'What is it that you are saying? That Achan doesn't love you?'

'Love isn't a service charge. It is a sense of completeness that someone finds in another person.'

This was directed at me.

'Please don't think I said that to dim your happiness. I am just giving you a heads-up. When I was your age, I thought family means heaven. After a while, I understood that this too is a workplace. A twenty-four-hour job. No leave, no promotion. Just a few small differences like that. At work, you might get a good service entry. At home, nothing you have ever done appears in the accounts. Only everything else you are supposed to do. I hope your life doesn't turn out that way. But don't forget that it could go that way. Don't be dejected.'

That was the only piece of advice my mother ever gave me. It proved to be useful in the very first couple of months of my marriage. Pramod didn't spend his time thinking of ways we could make each other happy. He was only intent on demonstrating how he was smarter than me. In the beginning, the friction was caused by the praise I received as a lawyer and a certain embarrassment about admitting it. So, my not getting pregnant right away turned into an all-encompassing crisis. The tests showed that the trouble lay at his end. Then began his paranoia. The short temper, the screaming fits and the prolonged sulks over the smallest things, and that time he slapped me in the face. And when, finally, a child was born after making the rounds of all those hospitals, it became clear that the problem wasn't the lack of a child.

Then it became about the child's behavioural problems. The second the doctor raised the possibility that Advaith might have Attention Deficit Hyperactive Disorder, the marriage that had been merely under the weather for years, coughed up blood and died on the spot. I had run to my mother then too. My mother said only one thing:

'Just remember what Tagore said: if you are inside the cage, there is no room to spread your wings, but you will have a perch to sit on. If you are in the sky, there is plenty of room to spread your wings, but no perch to sit on. Which is the one you want? You have to decide for yourself.'

I wasn't scared making that decision. Perhaps because the remaining perches in the cage had collapsed by then. My baby bird and I got out. Spread our wings and flew. I found a perch of my own to sit on—four years ago, when I passed the district judge selection exam on my very first attempt, I had got my quarters, a vehicle allowance, two office assistants, a life of security, a life with time for nothing other than work. I had been getting by. I had been okay. That's when Kaakkasseri Thangal made an entrance with Yogishwaran Ammavan.

I tucked Advaith in. Then I sat by the window. In three days, the moon would be full. The moonlight was brilliant. In the sky, a long-bearded white cloud carrying a silvery coconut was searching for someone.

I analysed the story of how the eldest nephew had got rid of Yogishwaran Ammavan. According to what my mother had told me, the nephew wasn't pleased by his ammavan's return. Who would be pleased at the prospect of going back to tail wagging when you have had five years of being ferried about on an elephant? At first, he dispatched a burly thug. Just one. Yogishwaran Ammavan pointed a finger at him and turned him into a statue. Assuming that Ammavan's powers lay in his index finger, the nephew knocked into him when Ammavan was lighting a lamp, ensured he burnt his finger and had to bandage it. This time the nephew sent four thugs. Yogishwaran Ammavan had studied Drishti Marmam. He just stared at them and turned them into statues. Next, the senior nephew served him poisoned milk gruel. Yogishwaran Ammavan brought it to his lips. The Elder Girl, who was inside the sacred grove, plucked a fruit from a jungle almond tree and chucked it, dashing the bowl of gruel from his grasp.

The senior nephew was enraged and released a crazed elephant in Ammavan's direction. The Younger Girl came swinging on a vine and calmed the elephant with a big bunch of bananas. Then the senior nephew released a thousand snakes into Yogishwaran Ammavan's room. The snakes slithered in reverse and disappeared into the grove. Those who went in their pursuit fainted at the sight of the Elder Girl who had snakes instead of hair. She cracked open and ate a fig as the snakes writhed against her. Later, the senior nephew sent a whole troop of men to attack Yogishwaran Ammavan while he lay sleeping. The hired guns tripped over the Younger Girl's vine and died.

One thing had become clear. Yogishwaran Ammavan's powers lay within the two girls. To kill him, they had to be destroyed. And there was only one way to destroy them—to feed them something touched by fire and rain. They bored a hole in a tender coconut, drained the juice and filled it with boiled water instead. One sip and the Elder Girl passed out. Her snakes died. The nephew's men caught her in a net. Took off her gold-trimmed dress. They dressed her in a gold-embroidered bodice, tied her hair up in a high bun, put heavy gold necklaces on her, and then nailed her to the yakshi pala tree in the sacred grove.

None of their tricks worked to get the Younger Girl down from the vine where she was half dozing. They gave the vine a great, catapulting swing and let it go. The vine swung out and the Younger Girl fell on the roof of a rich Jonakan's home eight hundred kilometres away. The Jonakan tycoon thought the girl who had fallen from the sky was a gift from Allah and shut her in the cellar. Made her wear a kaachi and thattam. To make sure no one outside would hear her cries, he inverted a huge copper cauldron over her. Every night, the Elder Girl with her golden clothes and heavy gold necklaces and high sideways bun writhed on the tree where she was nailed and cried out for her baby sister, 'Aniyathi!' Stuck under the cauldron, dressed in her kaachi and thattam and trapped by the chains around her ankles, the Younger Girl clamoured, 'Chechi!'

Now they were able to corner Yogishwaran Ammavan. The senior nephew leapt forward with a sword and a spear and first poked the old man's eyes out. Then he chopped off his fingers. He was about to behead the old man when Yogishwaran Ammavan asked for five minutes to pray, but they stabbed him to death anyway. In the middle of the courtyard, they had readied a hole twice the height of a man. There they buried him. To all those who came asking, they lied that Ammavan had returned to Kashi. Then a dog sped past those neighbours into the courtyard and clawed at the damp earth, whining all the while.

After that, no one in my father's family went to Kashi, no one's remains were immersed in the Ganga. At the southern end of the house, a tiny annexure was made with an ugly and inauspicious view from the window. The old uncles lay there on a sagging coir bed yelling, 'Rama, Krishna, Govinda, take me away soon.' And they died thirsty and parched.

I felt like Yogishwaran Ammavan's story was not just a story. There was a story of mine in there, one that I didn't recognise. A story that would be complete only with the melding of the Elder Girl nailed to the yakshi pala tree and the Younger Girl stuck under the copper cauldron. Kaakkasseri Thangal had entered my life to reveal this truth. But my eyes were blindfolded. I couldn't read what was written between the lines.

FOUR

Kaakkasseri Bhattathiri was destined to defeat outsider Brahmins. That was why he had been created. In those days, Manavikraman Shakthan Thampuran of Kozhikode organised a convention of great scholars once a year to get to the essence of the Vedas and Upanishads with ever more finesse. Splitting the Vedas, Shastras and Upanishads into a hundred and eight sections, the thampuran held debates about each section and gifted the winner of each debate a prize purse. The one hundred and ninth purse was for the oldest scholar. In the beginning, it was Malayali Brahmins who won all the money. But as word spread, Brahmins from elsewhere started coming to the competition. Soon it reached a stage where Malayalis weren't winning a single prize. Malayali Brahmins felt humiliated. They found a healthy and intelligent Brahmin woman and organised her marriage with a

Brahmin man who was both healthy and a scholar of the Vedas and Shastras. Through her pregnancy, they gave her potions and chanted mantras at her. An infant of great intelligence was born. At the age of three, he was initiated into writing. At five, he was given the sacred thread that would normally have been his only at the age of ten. Usually Samavartanam—the rite of passage when formal education ends for Brahmin boys—takes another three years. He finished that early too and began his brahmacharya, a phase of ascetic youth. Before childhood ended, he had mastered the essence of the Vedas, and had become a scholar and an eloquent orator. At the Tali temple in Kozhikode, where lighted lamps represented Prabhakara Mimamsa on the southern platform at the southern door, Bhatta Mimamsa on the northern end of the same platform, Vyakarana on the northern end of the northern platform and Vedanta on the southern end of the same platform, erudite debates were conducted. He strode into this annual assembly of scholars at the temple and single-handedly won all one hundred and nine purses. And thus the supremacy of Malayali Brahmins was re-established.

I felt curious about Kaakkasseri Bhattathiri, a man who had never been defeated in debate. I thought a lot about him. Perhaps Kaakkasseri Thangal had planted him in my mind. Because it was time now for my face-off with Kaakkasseri Thangal. That Monday morning, I had notified the cases for the next couple of days. I dictated them to Roshi and then asked:

'Roshi, is Mr Shyam Krishnan's daughter's baby a boy or a girl? Has he returned after seeing his grandchild?'

I didn't usually make small talk like that, so Roshi perked up. 'Madam, what I heard is that Shyam Sir will only return this morning,' he said. With that, the dam opened and out flowed all the gossip. Roshi had done all the necessary research on Kaakkasseri Khayaluddin Thangal. He recounted countless eyewitness testimonies of Thangal's sorcery and djinn worship. Here were some of the stories he had collected from Advocate Shyam Krishnan's juniors.

1. The first time that Kaakkasseri Thangal arrived in his office, Advocate Shyam Krishnan talked on the phone for a long time while Thangal sat before him. When he got bored, Thangal flicked an eyebrow. The lawyer looked at his phone without thinking. What he had pressed to his ear was not a phone. It was a small cobra. The lawyer panicked, screamed and threw the phone. It fell on the table. All his juniors came running. They all saw the small cobra, just the length of your palm, lying on the table.

Suddenly, it opened its mouth. Its forked tongue flickered in the rhythm of a phone's ringtone. Thangal picked it up without a care in the world and closed its mouth. He put it in his pocket and told the lawyer, 'Don't worry, sir. He won't bother you any more. We can talk now.' Shyam Krishnan became utterly abject. But even as they spoke, he couldn't stop looking at Thangal's pocket. When Thangal rose to leave, he took the cobra out of his pocket. Prised its mouth open and placed it on the table. The cobra became a phone again.

2. It was Kaakkasseri Thangal who drove Advocate Shyam Krishnan and his wife to the airport. When they saw the Marthanda Varma bridge in the distance, the lawyer said, 'We are lucky there is no blockage at the bridge.' Then Thangal asked, 'Bridge? What bridge?' When the lawyer and his wife looked again, the bridge wasn't there any more. The road was ending in mid-air. They screamed and tried to leap out of the moving car.
3. Thangal was beloved in his own village. He helped everyone tirelessly. Chanted folks' illnesses away. He was an architect. With projects abroad too.
4. Snakes were Thangal's familiars. Thangal was

reading a newspaper at the airport. A big, black cobra slithered up to him, crawled up his leg and into the folds of the newspaper. Everyone around him screamed. Thangal picked up the paper, rolled it up and walked away.

5. No one but he did sorcery in Kaakkasseri Thangal's family. Thangal had an uncanny ability to read other people's minds. He had been educated in Madras, Bombay, Delhi and other places. He spoke five or six languages fluently.

As I listened, my head swam. Was this man for real? I had never heard of or imagined a person or a life like that. But so what? The law was the law, and duty was duty. I looked at the calendar. Thursday was Independence Day. So I listed Kaakkasseri Thangal's case on Friday.

I was prepared. This time, immediately after roll call, I spotted him from the corner of my eye. Dark blue Nehru jacket. Sleeves rolled at the wrists and blue shirt tucked in. Formal pants. It was the first case of the afternoon. After lunch, I was back in my chair at 1.55 p.m. I pretended I couldn't see Advocate Shyam Krishnan's juniors rushing about, searching for their boss. Advocate Shyam Krishnan arrived panting, his paunch aquiver. It was a photo finish.

Our hot petitioner followed him. He bowed low. I didn't acknowledge it. I'd have to look him in the eye, wouldn't I, for him to plant a phantom in my mind?

The opposing counsel was Krishnakumar, who was my junior from law college. He was ready and waiting. Advocate Shyam Krishnan flung on his gown.

'Mister Counsel, your daughter had a baby, isn't that right?' I asked him.

'Yes, it's a boy.'

'Is she your only daughter?'

'She is our only child.'

'For her next pregnancy, Mister Counsel, you should bring your daughter home. Instead of doing voodoo on the judge and inconveniencing the other parties and lawyers,' I advised him politely.

His face became pale.

I asked, 'What about chief?'

Advocate Shyam Krishnan said, 'I have submitted an affidavit.'

But I could see that behind his gold-framed lenses, his initial confidence had faded. 'Let's begin chief,' I instructed.

The lawyer instructed the petitioner to step up to the stand and take oath. Even then, I ignored the petitioner.

Advocate Shyam Krishnan began the chief. 'Are you the one who submitted the affidavit?' 'Is everything you are saying in it true?' 'Is this signature yours?' and so on. He instructed the petitioner to look at the judge, bow and answer the questions.

Still I didn't look at him.

Since the petitioner's side didn't have any more questions, I asked for cross to begin. Advocate Krishnakumar stood up and came forward. He began his questions. Kaakkasseri Khayaluddin Thangal responded. I listened, keeping my mind calm and still.

'What is your ancestor's name?'

'Mohammed Askari Al Hasan Thangal.'

'Have you met him?'

'No.'

His voice had a quality of fearlessness. And sincerity.

'Have you spoken to, or met, anyone who has met him?'

'No.'

'Ah! So you have no exact information or even memory of Mohammed Askari Al Hasan?'

'The thing is, sir, our family history begins in 700 AD. A ship came from Arabia in 800 AD ...'

I intervened. I didn't look at the petitioner. Instead, I asked the opposing counsel, 'What is this? The viva section of your History of Kerala exam?'

Advocate Krishnakumar laughed sheepishly. He warned the petitioner, 'Please limit your answer to the question being asked. Do you have any exact information or even memory of Mohammed Askari Al Hasan?'

'No,' the petitioner replied in a slightly subdued voice.

'Then you admit that you have no proof that what you are calling a qabar belongs to your ancestor?'

'That is, 1,300 years ago, our …'

'Please. Just answer the question.'

'I admit it.'

'You are aware that the land on which you allege there is a qabar was bequeathed by your father to your brothers Salahuddin Thangal, Fasaluddin Thangal and Ameeruddin Thangal.'

'I am aware. But in the next survey number …'

'I didn't ask for the survey number. You can tell me the number when I ask for it. Of the two acres and fifteen cents of property, Nisaruddin Thangal willed seventy-five cents to Salahuddin Thangal, seventy-five cents to Fasaluddin Thangal and the remaining sixty-five cents to Ameeruddin Thangal. I have submitted the documents—the receipts, title deeds and transfer certificates. They sold the land to a charitable trust. The local panchayat, which does not have good halls for multi-faith weddings and public gatherings, has prepared the plans and estimates for an auditorium there. One with modern conveniences. That being so, doesn't your objection stand in the way of public interest? And even if you argue that the qabar has historical importance, you don't have any documents to prove it, do you?'

'When you say documents, do you mean ...'

'Do you have it or don't you?'

'I have no proof on paper.'

'Palm-leaf manuscripts then?'

'No. But just because there isn't a document doesn't mean there is no qabar.'

'Listen, just answer what you are asked, right? If there is a qabar, which side is the qiblah?'

'It will have to be measured.'

'In short, you don't know for sure if there is a qabar there. And if there is one, you don't know what kind of qabar.'

'No.'

'That's all, your honour.'

Advocate Krishnakumar bowed and retreated. I looked at Advocate Shyam Krishnan. He straightened his gold-rimmed glasses and came forward.

'What is your objection to an auditorium being built in this location?'

'This is the qabar of Hasan Koya, who had gone to Mecca with Cheraman Perumal, the Chera king, and returned having converted to Islam. The land where he lies is sacred to me. I have no objection to the auditorium being built. But I want the land where the qabar lies to be preserved. According to the current plan, the five toilets outside the auditorium are going to be built over the qabar.'

Advocate Shyam Krishnan looked at me as if to say, 'You heard that?'

I still didn't look at Thangal. But I shot Advocate Shyam Krishnan a hard glance.

'Mr Counsel, why are you dragging this out? Why don't you get to the point directly? This court has certain questions. Is there evidence to indicate that the land or location has history that goes back centuries, as the petitioner claims? Do any books of history refer to it?'

The courtroom grew utterly silent.

'If there is evidence, we can continue the argument. Else, let's close. The court is not the place for reciting Kerala history and someone's grandfather's woo-woo stories.'

I turned towards Advocate Krishnakumar.

'Does the opposing counsel want to do a re-cross?'

'No, your honour. We have submitted all the documents.'

'Do you have any witnesses?'

'No. Just documents.'

'So, the evidence is closed.'

The two lawyers agreed.

'So, the next date—alright, the next date will be 19 August,' I ordered. I put aside the papers and exhaled a little. Then, very carefully, I looked towards the witness stand. Kaakkasseri Khayaluddin Thangal, what magic do you have up your sleeve? What sorcery? He was emotionally wrecked. I could see that in his face. He looked at me sadly. I met that look with disinterest. Then the resentment surfaced on his face. His lips widened in a scornful smile. No novelty there. How many times had I seen that look and that smile, and how many times had I pretended not to see it to make it this far. He bowed and stepped out of the witness box, still holding my gaze. He went to the back of the courtroom and bowed to me again from the door. In all this time, I never looked away.

The next case was summoned. It was an appeal. The hearing began. Suddenly something twitched on my desk. A small cobra! It spread its hood right at the tip of my nose. I let out a small scream. And jumped up. Everyone in the courtroom rose. They all looked alarmed, wondering what had happened. It took me only a moment to come to my senses. I bowed and sat down again. I held my breath and said, 'Let us resume the hearing.' The snake was on my table. It looked at me, swaying its hood, threatening to strike any moment. I pretended not to see it. I leant back in my chair and tried to focus on the argument. My heart was pounding. I stole a look from the corner of my eye. That's when I realised my pen was missing. I picked up the snake with my sweat-drenched fingers. I wrote down what the petitioner had testified. The snake wrote better than a pen. Slowly, I let out my breath a little. Holding it between my fingers, I tapped my chin and looked obliquely towards the door. I saw Kaakkasseri Khayaluddin Thangal standing there. He looked shocked. Our eyes met again. I wrote down one more point with the snake. It became a pen again.

The hearing continued. I listened, absorbed. It was just about over when the closed window behind the witness stand opened gradually. Through the gap I saw the blue of Thangal's shirt. He picked up a piece of paper, looked at me and tore it in two. Then made a sound with his lips. Prprrrpprrrr. Not that I heard it. But I understood that was the sound he was making. In the blink of an eye, the window was closed again. It had taken just a moment. I heard that farting sound again. From my ... from my body! God! What a thing to happen! I jumped up. I ran to my chamber. Locked myself in the loo. I was scared. And embarrassed. I wanted to kill myself, I felt so humiliated. For several moments, I stood there sweating. I saw his face in front of me. Then I came to. I remembered that no one else had heard the sound and it was just in my head. Now I was enraged. I lost all self-control. I left my chamber and went outside to the veranda. I looked around. He was there. I stared straight into his eyes. I picked up a scrap of paper from the ground and tore it in two. I made that prrrrrrr sound with my lips. He stood paralysed. I went back inside, gnashing my teeth. I told Roshi to get me tea. I drank the tea, returned to my seat and trudged through the rest of my cases.

I was wiped out. On the way back to my quarters, the car drifted several times. The steering wheel seemed like a coiled, twisted serpent. I felt like crying. I felt vengeful towards the whole world. Turning towards the quarters, I hit the accelerator instead of the brake and almost slammed the wall on the left side. I swerved. The car got dinged just above the left wheel. Only inside the house did I finally relax.

Manju was feeding Advaith dinner. I made some perfunctory gestures of affection and went into my bedroom. I had a quick bath and collapsed onto my bed. My head hurt as if it was going to split open. My mind was suffused with the bitterness of that afternoon's humiliation. I despised Kaakkasseri Khayaluddin Thangal. FilthyBarbarianCreep, I ranted to myself. Just then, someone rang the doorbell. Manju came in a little later to say, 'Madam, there is a letter.'

'A letter? At this time?' I asked, and opened the envelope. Inside was a wedding card torn in two. The pieces shook in my hands. An invitation to the wedding of the person I had loved with all my heart from the time I was twenty. It would have had the power to make me cry anyway. It was the qabar of love, of dedication, of lost virtues and unfulfilled hopes. My heart trembled. But it wasn't the card that made me cry. It was what was written below 'with compliments': 'Prrrprrrrprrr'.

I was still crying when Advaith returned from his cycling. I struggled to hide my tears. No, I wasn't crying for love. Love doesn't have the power to make you cry so much. But humiliation does. I was incandescent with rage. Gnashing my teeth, I wrote Kaakkasseri Thangal's judgement in my head.

That night, as I lay next to a sound-asleep Advaith, as I tossed and turned and lay on my side and back and front, the girl nailed to the yakshi pala tree and the girl trapped under the cauldron, both writhed inside me. I was afraid they would kill and eat each other. I hated myself. I wanted to kill and eat myself.

FIVE

And then it was 19 August. The day of Kaakkasseri Khayaluddin Thangal's next hearing. Out of curiosity, I had looked up Kaakkasseri Bhattathiri and read a little more. Kaakkasseri Bhattathiri had been created by the local Brahmins to beat the outsiders. Winning was his destiny, not the development of epistemology. Silence his opponents—that was all they wanted. Bhattathiri, a man programmed to only debate, practised beginning his responses to anything any scholar said with 'Nahin, nahin, no, no'. Hearing the endless iterations of nahin-nahin, an eminent scholar was annoyed and pronounced, 'tava mata pativrata'. Bhattathiri responded to the endorsement of his mother's fidelity by saying 'nahin-nahin' as a matter of course. The eminent scholar laughed. Recognising the trap, Bhattathiri was thrown. Then he recited a shloka:

'Soma: prathamo vividhe gandharvo vividha uttara:
Tathriyo agnishte pathi: thuriyasthe manushyaja:'

And thus escaped by the skin of his teeth.

'When a woman is born, first she is the moon's. Then the gandharvan gets her. Then fire gets her. It is only then, with fire as her witness, that the man who marries her gets her.' That was the approximate meaning of what he said. The eighth ashtaka of the Rig Veda. Third chapter. Twenty-seventh varga. Fifth shloka.

Kaakkasseri Bhattathiri had been a scholar since childhood. And every year, he had acquired more and more scholarship. He discovered more analyses of the Upanishads. Then? There is a limit to scholarship. And that limit is the average intelligence of the majority of society. A higher than average intelligence and scholarship has always been a pain in the ass for society. And Bhattathiri? When he studied more, he learnt that there was no such thing as a foreigner. And when he studied some more, he learnt that there was no such thing as an original inhabitant. When he studied even more, he realised there was no such thing as the other. And then that there was no such thing as the self.

By then, some of the Brahmins had lost their patience. Without purity, untouchability and tradition, what was society? What meaning did the competition have then? What meaning the prize purse? They asked Bhattathiri and learnt from him how he could be destroyed. Then they drew magic circles, lit lamps and did rituals for the goddess. They chanted mantras for forty days. On the forty-first day, Bhattathiri arrived at the site of the yajna. They gave him water to drink. He drank the water, turned the vessel upside down and said, 'I am an outcaste right now. I won't come closer. I won't touch you.' Then he left. No one ever saw him after that. No one knew where he had gone. Where did he die? When did he die? No one ever found out.

Where was Kaakkasseri Bhattathiri headed? How had Bhattathiri become bhrasht, become an outcaste, so he couldn't go near the yajna? I was disturbed by the path he had taken. The man who had climbed to the peak of scholarship. The man who had come to know that knowing what you don't know is knowledge, the man who had turned upside down the vessel of his knowledge and left on his journey, would that man not have gone in search of the spring of unknown knowledge? I was deeply unsettled.

Anyway, Kaakkasseri Khayaluddin Thangal's hearing proceeded beautifully. I was scheduled to pronounce the verdict on the second. Even on the morning of 2 September, I felt energetic. After all, it was the day of Pramod's wedding. Should I go to the wedding or not? I had subjected myself to a cross-examination long back. I had arguments and counter-arguments. On one side was justice. On the other side was the law. In some cases, the petitioner wins by allowing an ex-parte respondent to win. In other cases, the petitioner wins by not appealing against a verdict that is favourable to the respondent. Throwing dust in the eyes of love, making the soul blind, nailing me to the yakshi pala tree of society—that was what my marriage had done. When the wood rotted, the nails fell down, one by one. There was one last one. And Advaith had removed that one too. One has to thank the sorcerer for everything you get sitting inside the magic circle, for the frenzied dancing, for being beaten with canes, for being impaled with nails. Else, how would the fate of the embattled soul be determined? The sorcerer's soul too was in the fray. And without recognising that, the 'lack of empathy' wouldn't be cured. I decided to go to the wedding.

On Saturday, Advaith and I went into town. We bought new clothes. After all, it was the wedding of someone I had once adored, wasn't it? If we weren't well dressed, wouldn't the public read our minds? Plus, after the wedding, I had to go and preside over my courtroom. So, I bought a sari that would work in both places and would go with a black high-necked blouse. The muhoortam was between 9 and 9.30 a.m.

And the bride's home was in my jurisdiction. Both were helpful in getting me to court in time after the event. If the muhoortam had been between 12 and 2 p.m., I would have been stuck. I would have had to take the day off. All the lawyers and judges who didn't attend the wedding would have assumed that I was crying at home, unable to face people because my ex-husband was getting married.

When I told Advaith that he didn't have to go to school, he raised a ruckus. When he found out it was to go to his father's wedding, he objected. 'I don't want to go', 'I don't want to see him', 'Don't make me go', he kept yelling. But I didn't relent. At some point, he would, like me, have to see Pramod with his new wife. The sooner it happened, the better. I closed my eyes and counted. One, two, three, four. When I got to thirty-five, he wiped his eyes and came to me. He was persuaded by the argument that if he didn't go with Amma, there was no one else to go with Amma. He agreed to come along. We reached the auditorium exactly at 9 a.m. I had lucked out, I suppose! The tying of the thali, the exchange of rings, the garlanding and the groom giving the bride a sari—it all went off well.

Elbowing my way to my husband's wedding feast—that was a bit much. I decided to abstain from the lunch. I went over to wish the couple. As soon as they saw me, lawyers stepped aside from the queue.

Pramod's mother was the first to spot us. Her thickly made-up face darkened. Her face did that whenever she saw me. So I paid no attention. But when she saw my child, she turned away abruptly. That was like a stab in the heart. My blood boiled. I didn't dawdle after that. I went straight up to the bride and groom. Pramod blanched like he had seen a ghost. He seemed about to faint. It was an act of cruelty towards him to have gone to his wedding. But it would have been an act of cruelty towards me to not have gone.

My ex-husband's new wife was a good woman. 'I wanted to come and speak to you before, madam. But I wondered whether you wouldn't like it, so I didn't.' And such-like banter. 'Is this Advaith,' she asked before caressing him. Advaith clutched my hand and clamoured, 'Let's leave, let's leave.' I looked Pramod in the eye and congratulated him. He looked deflated. And thus I drew my last drop of water from that particular well, drank it and turned the vessel upside down. Duty done, I departed.

So far so good. Once we got in the car, my calculations went awry. Advaith threw a tantrum about going home. He found it impossible to focus on anything. He could throw a fit, oblivious to his surroundings. So, taking him to court was a risk. But that day, I decided to let Roshi and Selina handle him till noon. When I fastened my band and collar and put on my gown, Advaith was frightened and yelled. Eventually Roshi picked him up and took him outside. That must have been when he came on Kaakkasseri Thangal's radar. I had seen him before roll call. A sea-green kurta and churidar. A white silk Nehru jacket. But I quickly drew my gaze away. When I read the judgement, I did not look at him at all. After all, if there was another prrrprrr sound, I would be decimated. I didn't waste any time. Right away, I read out the summary of my verdict.

The petitioner's brothers, respondents one to three, of their own volition, have given the property to a charitable trust which intends to make it useful for all sections of society. The petitioner is unable to submit documents or produce witnesses who can establish that there is indeed a tomb on the property that is allegedly that of his ancestor. The petitioner has been unable to establish that the public utility building is being constructed by encroaching on this tomb. Since the petitioner has been unable to establish his allegations, I am ordering the case dismissed. I am also rejecting the request for a stay order.

As soon as I finished reading out the verdict, I felt lighter. I became more energetic. There were two more appeal hearings. When one o'clock rolled around, I didn't even register it. Only when Selina indicated that it was time, did I notice. I finished the procedures in a hurry and went to my chambers. Advaith wasn't there. Roshi wasn't in his seat either. I guessed that Advaith was with Roshi. But just then Roshi appeared, wiping his hands, on his way back from the canteen. I asked, 'Where is the kid?' Roshi looked at Selina, and Selina looked at Roshi. For a moment, we were all terrified. But then we heard that jangly laughter of his. I saw him on the landing of the staircase at the end of the corridor, standing in front of the Motor Vehicle Tribunal office. Kaakkasseri Khayaluddin Thangal was amusing him with magic tricks. Passersby looked in amazement as he plucked bouquets out of thin air and made toffees rain from his palm. Just then, he spotted me. He pointed me out to Advaith and said something. Advaith came running straight to me. And hugged me. I smothered my irritation and took him inside the chamber. Then he stretched out the arm he had held behind him. It was a bouquet. A bouquet of Edward roses. He brushed my cheek with it. My body felt electrified. There is no law against judges feeling electrified. Nothing to stop them from having ancient qabars buried in their heart. If someone demolished one of those qabars, that someone did not have to be taken to court. No rule that one shouldn't feel destroyed by the sight of the corpse of love lying there, still bleeding.

This must be the Illusion of the Day. I felt

exhausted. My mind felt fuzzy. I was my body, which had just divorced my mind. My memories of the loving moments I had with Pramod became djinns flying all around me. I decided to take the afternoon off. I took Advaith out to a restaurant. And then to a movie. The movie was called *Ambili*. Since it was daytime on a weekday, there was hardly anyone. Advaith was jubilant. He climbed up on his seat to sing along with a song in the movie. Applauded loudly. The person sitting next to him clapped along. After that, I didn't catch any of the film. I sat there and melted away. Wasn't there a moment when the Elder Girl nailed to the yakshi pala tree and the Younger Girl trapped under the cauldron met again? That's how I felt. Reunited, they found Yogishwaran Ammavan. The dog that my father had censored from the story, the dog that my mother had reanimated, saw the sisters and somersaulted in happiness. That was the happiness I experienced.

Yogishwaran Ammavan had gone to Kashi after he had seen a thousand full moons. Why had he come back? Perhaps because, until then, he hadn't seen the moon, the night and moonlight. For five years on the road, in inns, in graveyards, in monasteries, temples and ghats, he must have experienced true nights, real darkness and the destabilising magic of moonlight. After tramping through rocky patches and thorny brush and distant lands, after hearing many languages spoken, after fording many rivers, he must have discovered that life is not a suit, it's a decree. Must have understood that God is nobody's judge, he is everyone's witness. Must have accepted that religion is the search for spiritual bliss. And then he must have bathed in the Ganga. Stretched out on the steps of the ghats, where corpses smouldered, when he understood what his ancestors who had arrived there before him had been in search of, he must have laughed. He must have slept to his heart's content. And when he woke, he must have set out to journey somewhere else. Two girls—orphaned by those who could never have enough land, those never soothed by religion, those lusting for blood—must have begged him, 'Take us with you.'

That movie was also the story of the journey of two people. Long roads and mountains shimmered on the screen. I saw that it wasn't the foreign girls who were walking along holding Yogishwaran Ammavan's hands. It was Advaith and me. At some point, Yogishwaran Ammavan became Kaakkasseri Khayaluddin Thangal. He sat between Advaith and me. I forgot how close a petitioner and the judge who had dismissed his case were allowed to sit.

'Madam, I ask for your forgiveness,' he said. In the darkness, we looked at each other. It was mesmerising.

The light from the screen turned his eyes into jewels. This time, there were no rainbows. Just brilliance. Like a lake at noon. Like the sea in the moonlight.

'Want a pen to turn into a snake?' I asked. He whispered again, 'Forgive me.' That whisper came from his heart. It held a trace of scorn for himself so I held back my next question, 'Do you want some paper to tear into two?'

'Do you have djinns who are your slaves?' I asked.

'They are not slaves, they are friends,' he laughed.

'Can you make them do anything you want?'

'Anything that they think is right.'

'Can you make me invisible?'

'We are already invisible now.'

'Can you teach me magic?'

'But you must give me the fee I ask for.'

'I will,' I promised easily. Suddenly, in the movie theatre, a cauldron flipped over, enveloping him and me in darkness. Inside, only his eyes and mine shone bright. I learnt that the biggest feat of magic in the world is how the pupils of a man and a woman gazing at each other turn into diamonds. Before he could ask me for a fee for that lesson, I made an offering—a deep kiss on his lips, a kiss that contained a spell.

SIX

Before setting out, I left Advaith at my mother's house. In the car, Kaakkasseri Khayaluddin Thangal asked me, 'Madam, what did you say to your mother?' I found that an interesting detail about him. After the first time we kissed, Pramod had never called me anything other than 'edi'. The kiss established his right to that form of address. But that was a clueless phase. I mistook the 'edi' for a promotion—like the munsif being elevated to Chief Justice of the Supreme Court. I gloated about it.

I had been sure that Kaakkasseri Thangal would take revenge for having to bow and scrape in front of me in court. I had prepared myself to deal with that moment when it came. As if he had read my mind, he became even more submissive and polite. That scared me.

'Amma didn't ask me anything. She must have assumed I am going to a training,' I said.

'There is no training in sorcery. Only devotion.'

He looked at me, tapping a beat on the steering wheel. 'Do you know why, madam?'

'Explain it to me.'

'This is an art form. All arts involve give-and-take of emotions between people. There is no training for any emotional transaction. Only devotion. What you need to learn is that it is not a deliberate decision, it is an inspired intuition.'

It began to rain. It was raining flowers. I was bewildered. I rolled down the window and looked up. The sky had turned pink. Flowers fell, knocking against my nose and throat. They fell from a great height. Some petals were crushed and made my face damp. I laughed in a jangly way, like Advaith. I hooted and crowed, totally forgetting that I was a judge. All the hatred I had felt towards Kaakkasseri Khayaluddin Thangal was knocked aside by those flowers. The roses had piled into tiny mountain ranges and the road had transformed into a pink carpet. Kaakkasseri Thangal—dressed in a yellow Nehru jacket and a kurta-pyjama with yellow embroidery at the collar—drove his Rolls-Royce Ghost on this long road. The wheels of the car didn't touch the road. Didn't crush a flower. The flowers that fell through the open window piled up in my lap. I scooped them up and inhaled their fragrance.

'How long will you keep up this illusion?' I was anxious.

'As long as madam permits it.'

Slowly, the shower of roses ended. Only a large rose that had tangled in my hair remained. I was lovelorn.

'Why do you call me madam, instead of calling me by my name?'

'What you need is respect. And that is what you haven't been getting.'

My anxiety disappeared. What qabar was he preparing to demolish? I became careful.

'And that is true for me too,' he added.

'But you are rich, influential, and above all, a man!' I protested.

'That's me on the outside.'

My heart swelled up.

'On the inside, I am none of that. I am a man who has experienced a riot. Once a huge mob strips you naked and looks at your genitals to find out which side you are? No one to whom that has happened—whether you are a Hindu or a Muslim—stays a person.'

I was stunned. This was completely unexpected. Until then I was just a judge and a woman seduced by a man. But in that moment, I was Hindu and he was Muslim. In that moment, I was also afraid of him.

'Madam, say the girl nailed to the yakshi pala and the girl trapped under the cauldron meet. Would the older sister be afraid of her younger sister? Would the younger sister hate her older sister?' he asked. I wanted to escape. Kaakkasseri Thangal wasn't just my nemesis. He was a nemesis with the ability to read your mind. My confidence was shaken. The weighing scales of my mind rocked wildly from side to side. I struggled to grab and steady them.

'How do you know the story of the Older Girl and the Younger Girl?' I swallowed hard.

'In sorcery, what we control is other people's imagination. That is, we control *bhavana*. So, a little homework is mandatory.'

I looked at him. He tapped out a beat on the steering wheel. A big butterfly with blue wings sat on the windscreen. It looked at me and smiled. It winked at me. I sat there, terrified. It smiled wider, spread its wings and flew away. My terror doubled.

'I'd believe you if you said you had done your homework on me. But how could you possibly manipulate my imagination without knowing for sure that I knew that story?'

He laughed. Tapped out that beat again. The steering wheel became a serpent. A gold serpent with dark red eyes. It looked at me and twinkled its eyes at me. I stretched my hand out to the snake. Kaakkasseri held that hand and brought it to his lips. Brushed his well-shaped beard against my palm. I felt ticklish and withdrew my hand.

He slowly drove into a lane. On one side of the lane were rubber farms. On the other side, a tree-filled compound. I was afraid that his large car would get scratched up by the walls in that narrow lane. But he skilfully drove up and parked alongside a fence. From a textiles store bag on the backseat, he pulled out a purdah that looked new and handed it to me.

'What is this for?' I was unnerved.

'The judge and the petitioner in the case shouldn't be seen together, right?' He laughed. My throat grew even more parched. He offered me water. I drank a mouthful. Then opened up the purdah.

'Why does the magician need a purdah? Can't you hypnotise people into imagining that I am invisible?' I mocked him as I pulled on the purdah and stepped out of the car.

'The hypnotist is like a poet. The poet worships the poem. The poem invites the poet. In the same way, my illusions don't work on anyone who doesn't invite them.'

He looked at me. His eyes glittered like that first day. I pulled down the veil and covered my eyes. He smiled and said, 'Madam, please come along.' I looked around. We were in a compound filled with big trees and vines. The whole property was overcast with a green darkness. Why had this man brought me here? If he buried me in this desolate little forest, who would ever find me? I felt nervous.

'Don't worry. Nothing like that is going to happen now that we have CCTVs on every street,' he said.

'I want to learn to read minds too,' I said with some embarrassment.

'It's best that you don't. Since I learnt to read minds, I have never been able to stay in any relationship.' He smiled sadly.

'When I began mind-reading, it was kind of fun. After reading the minds of my siblings and the girl I was in love with, I regretted learning how to.'

We walked through the trees. We could see construction going on in the next plot. He walked towards it. Three JCBs were clawing at the earth. A wall had risen like a scar in that tree-filled land.

'This is my boundary.'

He pointed out a spot on the wall. My heart raced. Had he brought me here to show me that I had made a mistake?

'This is where the qabar is.' He moved aside a crumpled tarpaulin. I saw the broken pieces of two small minarets.

'What evidence do you have that this is where the qabar is?' My voice was filled with irritation.

'Shouldn't the court help prove it?' He looked at me helplessly.

'Shouldn't documents and evidence be submitted for that?'

'We are taught that history is part of the inheritance of all of mankind, aren't we? I believed, wrongly, that this was a case I could win easily. That was what my lawyer had me believe too.' He smiled unhappily.

'I didn't know that my younger brothers had sold the land. But perhaps they had no other option. Their business had run into losses. It looked like this land would be foreclosed. It was a distress sale. The trust promised to buy the land. They agreed. They informed me after signing the agreement.'

'And if you had known earlier?'

'I would have bought the land the qabar sits on somehow.'

'Didn't your brothers know about this qabar?'

'What did the qabar matter while they were battling life-and-death issues? As soon as I found out, I called Salahuddin. By then, it had already been sold.'

'Couldn't you have told the buyers to just set aside this portion of the land?'

'That is the mistake I made. I called the trust that had bought the land. I told them that there is a qabar here. I requested them to sell me just enough land to keep the qabar safe, at a premium of 10,000 rupees for each cent. The secretary of the trust asked for a week to think about it. The next thing I knew, they had started building the wall. They must have been scared that Muslims would make trouble if word got out that there was a qabar here.'

He walked back. He opened the car door. He drove the car out of the compound and then stepped out to close the gate. Back in the driving seat, he asked, 'Aren't you taking off the purdah?' I took it off, folded it, put it back in the plastic bag and returned it to the backseat. We didn't speak till we were back on the main road. My chest felt heavy.

'Chheh! My mistake. I was prejudiced,' I said, faltering.

'It was my fault too. I was prejudiced too. In any case, when one has one setback after the other, one becomes very prejudiced.'

'Did your mesmerism not work on the secretary of the trust?'

His face fell.

'If I wanted to break the law, I had endless ways to do it, but I have never used my talents for anything other than to help or please someone.'

'And what you did to me?'

'That was because of my lawyer's tears.' He let out a deep sigh. 'But that wedding card, that was me testing you.' His voice became anxious. His face was flushed and his eyes gleamed with tears.

My heart sped. I worried that this was my own illusion. The car was filled with a heavy silence.

'In this case, it will be hard to get an injunction from a higher court. The evidence that the other side submitted is very strong.' I tried to change the subject.

'Let's see.'

'Don't be stupid enough to think you can win the case by reading the mind of the judge in the higher court.'

'Then let me tell you a truth. I never read the mind of anyone who doesn't want their mind read.'

'Meaning?'

'Reading minds is not a pleasant activity, madam. It's hard to look at a dissected body, even if it is that of a world-class beauty. '

I was a bit shocked.

'And another thing. After a while, you realise most people are the same. The same hopes, greed, disappointments, insecurities.'

'Nevertheless, I want to read your mind.'

'Madam, you read my mind long ago. Haven't you already begun to manipulate it?' His cheeks reddened. I liked that.

'Did you file an appeal?' I asked.

'I did. It's been posted for two days from today.'

'What if it's rejected? What will you do?'

'Go to the higher court.'

'Before that, make sure that some newspaper prints that a qabar that goes back to 8 AD has been found on the Kaakkasseri estate,' I said.

'And then?'

'Give a letter to the archaeological department that you have found this qabar.'

'And then?'

'Then nothing. You can relax because they will take over the qabar and the land it sits on.'

'And then?'

I didn't answer. He was the one who said:

'Madam, this is a personal joy of mine. The person who lies beneath that qabar is someone who, centuries ago, loved and was loved, was cheated and died. I sprung and grew from that root. That's why it is significant to future generations too. It's not about religion, it's about family. Any kind of publicity will bring on the believers. I don't want that.'

'So, what are you going to do?'

'I will take it as far as it can go. After that ... whatever the court decides.'

I felt guilty. For a long while, we were silent. The return journey was quick. He stopped the car at the beginning of the street that turned towards my mother's house. Before I got out, I asked, 'What did you read in my mind?'

His answer was short.

'Madam, you are not one person. You are two.'

He held my hand and looked at me with a kind of admiration that no one had shown before.

'Two. The girl who made ornaments of snakes. And the girl who sat on a vine and swung into the sky.'

I wanted to weep. For the first time in my life, I felt a sense of completeness in someone else's company.

SEVEN

There was, in fact, a legend about my birth. My mother became pregnant with me five years after my brother was born. Till the fifth month, there were two babies in her womb. But in the sixth month, only one heartbeat was audible. And during labour, only I emerged. Once, some relative of my father's told me that I had eaten my twin. I was shell-shocked. 'Did I really eat the little baby?' I asked my mother many times. My mother explained that babies in the womb can't eat like that and they get nutrients in the bloodstream through the umbilical cord from their mother. I wasn't satisfied. The mother of one of my high-school classmates was a doctor. One day, when I saw her waiting for her daughter, leaning against her Maruti Esteem car, I went up to her. 'Doctor, can I ask a doubt?' I asked nervously. Her gaze raked me up and down. Her face was unreadable.

'If you want a consultation, come to the hospital after ten tomorrow,' she said.

'It's not a consultation. I just had a doubt. If there are two babies in a mother's stomach, can just one baby go away?'

She looked at me and frowned.

'Yes. It's called a vanishing twin.'

By then, her daughter arrived. The doctor jumped in her car and they sped away. I didn't feel bad. My cheap clothes, my sweat-streaked face—it was a big deal that she had said as much as she had. When I got a computer and an internet connection of my own, I looked it up—the vanishing twin syndrome. That's when the reason for my perpetual restlessness became clear. I had never been just myself. On the outside, I was the girl swinging on the vine. On the inside, the girl who ate the endless fruit of the yakshi pala, who wore the snakes of the yakshi pala as ornaments, who was nailed to the yakshi pala, that girl had merged into her. She hadn't disappeared. As long as one existed, neither would disappear.

The day that I went to see the site of the qabar with Kaakkasseri Khayaluddin Thangal was 9 September 2019. The next day was Uthradam, the ninth day of Onam. I went to my father's house. On the next day, on Thiruvonam, as usual, my mother came home to eat lunch. And, as usual, I went back with her. Then, in the afternoon, my older brother, his wife, their children and my father came to my mother's house. They took Advaith along for a trip to Mahabalipuram. I stayed with my mother and my mother's thirty-two children. Shook out and dusted her books. Wiped clean her delegate badges from union conventions. Read a couple of books. The thought that someone who read my mind was reading the book along with me, was thrilling. I read some passages aloud for him. I re-read some bits.

It was 15 September when Advaith returned. From the next day, life returned to its regular, well-worn grooves. On the twenty-third, as I walked from the parking lot to court, I saw Advocate Shyam Krishnan. He greeted me. We made small talk.

'Have you appealed the qabar case?' I enquired.

'We got a two-month injunction.'

'What's two months?' I smiled.

'When the client says that's all he wants, what are we to say?'

I didn't enquire any further. Advocate Shyam Krishnan said goodbye. I felt anxious as I walked towards my chambers. I hadn't learnt to read Kaakkasseri Thangal's mind. But he was able to read mine. That whole day, he invaded my mind. I only thought of him. Why had he decided that he wanted only a two-month injunction? Why hadn't he come to see me? Was he bored of reading my mind? Was my mind so shorn of substance that just a car ride worth of mind-reading had bored him?

The next day, when I arrived at my chambers, there on my table was a large bouquet of Edward roses. And that night, when I lay down to sleep, on the ceiling was a blue butterfly with sparkling eyes. After that, every day, a bouquet arrived on my table. And every night, the blue butterfly fluttered its eyes at me from its perch on the ceiling. My soul was filled with the peace that comes from feeling completed by someone else. The girl who swung on the vine swung from the rosewood tree to the teak tree and from the teak tree to the sky.

I longed feverishly to see him. The lines that remained unread in my mind unsettled me. And then it was October. On the second, I was getting ready to go to my mother's house. After saying goodbye to Selina, I locked the house and turned around to find the red Rolls-Royce at my gate. I felt my feet levitate and then the rest of me floated in air. Advaith caught sight of him and ran towards him in glee. He showered Advaith with flowers and butterflies. Made him fly though he had no wings. Made him walk upside down in mid-air till he collapsed, laughing. Then he picked up Advaith and held out his hand to me. A big Edward rose bloomed at the tip of his finger. I tucked it into my hair.

The journey was unworldly. He drummed on the steering wheel. The car rose into the clouds. The clouds shone silver. When he honked the horn, the clouds stepped aside. When he shone the headlights, the clouds turned yellow. When he drummed that beat again, we were in a valley of blue daisies. The road ahead turned blue. It was the road to the High Range. It rained on the way. The rain spun golden threads. The path was dusted with gold and the mountain ranges were golden. In a while, the rain stopped. It was twilight. The road was paved with gems. Advaith expressed a desire to fly in the sky. So, we flew again. The receding sun polished the sky gold. He leapt and somersaulted among saffron and red clouds. He soon grew tired and fell asleep in the backseat. I reached out and touched Thangal's hand on the steering wheel. He leant down and kissed my hand.

'Madam, I have read and read and read your mind, but I haven't got my fill, ' he said.

I looked at him with annoyance. 'Where have you been?' I asked.

'I was building a house.'

'You were building it yourself?'

'Yes. Me. All by myself. I have built many homes for other people before. But this is the first time I am building a house for myself.'

'What happened to the case?'

'I have time till next month,' he smiled.

He took us to a house on a mountain top, a house that had sprung up like a mushroom in the shadow of a rock that stuck out against the sky. This was the house he had built. Its facade was made of a single white marble stone. What is this, the Taj Mahal, I mocked him. He pointed to the name carved into the gate. Bhavana. I was shaken. My eyes filled with tears and my vision blurred. I tried to believe that this was an illusion. I felt defeated. Exhausted. Why had he named the house Bhavana? Was it just a word that he liked? Was it another trick? The house had five bedrooms. Why so many? I was puzzled. What if it becomes necessary, he smiled. He made us a meal. I searched the house with a fine-tooth comb. I looked everywhere for evidence of his secret life. He teased me, saying that there was nothing to be found on the outside. As for what was on the inside, I was free to read it all, he said, throwing down the gauntlet.

Advaith fell asleep as soon as he had eaten. We switched off the lights and sat outside on the veranda. It was dark as far as the eye could see. The sound of crickets grew and grew. The butterfly tree next to the gate glittered with lakhs of invading fireflies. It turned into a tree with golden scales where there should have been leaves. When the tree swayed in the breeze, I imagined that they were the tiny golden hairs of the mane of an Arabian horse. Was it also an illusion, I wondered. But it wasn't. Because he was more intoxicated than I was. He was wondering whether it was an illusion I had made. That was the first whole sentence I read in his mind.

After that, I had no difficulty. I read his whole mind. It was fun in the beginning. Like reading Neruda, Hemingway and Rumi. In a while, though, the language changed. The words changed. The emotions changed. His mind became the stories of Saadat Hasan Manto. I hurt. Some pages were soaked in my tears. Some pages scorched my eyes. I stopped reading at the penultimate page. My endless guilt over having devoured my twin in the womb rose again. I wanted to ask forgiveness. He fell into my arms and wept. That broke my heart.

For him, I became a tree that was dusted with gold from the crown to the roots. And then a jungle jasmine heavy with stars. And then a river of moonlight and a garden of fireflies. I became a fire-breathing dragon and gold melted in the furnace. The night stretched out, a never-ending book. At dawn, he began his sorcery again. A shower of flowers and a spring of butterflies. Stars leaping out of flowers and moonlight at high noon. Silver birds with blue eyes and golden serpents with coral eyes. Then the breeze, coolness, dizzying fragrances.

The next evening, we drove down the mountain. As soon as we got into the car, Advaith fell asleep. We read each other's minds and laughed. The Rolls-Royce flowed without touching the road strewn with red flowers.

'When will I see you again?' I asked without asking.

'On 9 November,' he said without speaking.

'And then?' I asked without asking. He concealed that page in his mind from me so I couldn't read it. I tried to grab it. He hid it again mischievously. That night, I didn't feel like Advaith and I were alone. He was in my hair, in my body and at my fingertips. He was in my heart and my womb.

The next day, I set out for court half-heartedly. Before I entered my chambers, the fragrance of Edward roses welcomed me. Every bit of me was now wide awake. A terracotta pot with a hundred flowers smiled at me from my desk. Wasn't a single flower enough? I felt embarrassed. At night, a hundred butterflies arrived on the ceiling. Wasn't one enough? I was overjoyed. After that, every day, flowers stood in full bloom on my table. And every night, blue butterflies crinkled their eyes at me and smiled. Every now and then, someone stepped right into my mind and recited poetry. I imprisoned him. He remained tangled inside me. I was waiting for 9 November.

I woke up early. The morning was brighter than

usual. I felt a great urgency and impatience. I woke Advaith, bathed him and sent him to badminton classes with Manju. I had a case for which the High Court had set a time limit. I had told Roshi to come to work even though it was a holiday. As I stepped out with my bag and my keys, I saw a car draw up at the gate. My father and three others. 'You have a sitting even though it's a second Saturday?' my father asked as he stepped in.

Seeing that I was in a hurry, they said what they had come to say without any preamble.

'We are organising the restoration and re-consecration of the Kaakkarakunnu Devi temple. For the multi-faith meeting that day, madam, you must come as our chief guest. It's not like other temples. People from all religions are allowed to enter.'

'Do you know which temple this is?' my father intervened.

'You remember I had told you about Yogishwaran Ammavan the other day? You know, Varma saar, in the old days, the heads of our household used to go to Kashi when they were old. They would either die during the journey or they would pass away in Kashi. Only one uncle ever came back. And that was Yogishwaran Ammavan. His eldest nephew washed his face one morning, looked out into the yard and there he was, his uncle. And with him were two little girls who looked like goddesses. After the nephew washed Ammavan's feet, when he turned to the children, what do you think he saw? The girls' feet didn't touch the ground. He took the children to the auspicious south-western corner and sat them on the korandi. They had to be fed, right? That's when they said—we don't eat anything touched by fire or rain. He ran off to chop down a tender coconut. But when he came back with a coconut under each arm, were the children there? Both were missing. He called out loudly: Older One, Younger One! The older one heard his calls from our yakshi pala tree in the sacred grove. The younger one heard his call from the Jonakan's house eight hundred kilometres away, from under a cauldron. The goddess who heard the call from under the cauldron, that's the Kaakkara Devi.'

My heart raced.

'And Yogishwaran Ammavan?' I asked.

'In those days, the household was a mansion, right? In the courtyard was a pit. He stumbled and fell in. No one saw him falling. And that is how Yogishwaran Ammavan died.' My father said all this with definiteness. But I remembered what my mother had said.

I sent them on their way, saying things like, let me see, I will let you know. I left for court immediately. My heart was quaking. Where was my magician? How and when was he going to appear before me? Even though it was a holiday, I expected the spring of Edward roses in my chambers. But when I got there, forget spring, there wasn't a single flower. I was shattered. The terracotta vase sat there with its mouth agape. I noticed for the first time that it was a small burial jar. And something was entombed in it. Some unknown terror slammed against the walls of my heart. I writhed in pain.

Advocate Krishnakumar arrived just then.

'Bhavana chechi. Good morning ...'

'Good morning, Krishna. How come you are here on a holiday?' I pretended to be happy to see him.

'I was setting out for your quarters. That's when I saw your car coming in.'

He handed me an invitation card. 'I have built a small house. This is for the housewarming next Sunday. You must come and you must bring your son. The address is at the back of the card. It's just five kilometres from here.'

'I will come for sure,' I promised. While Krishnakumar chatted about this and that, my mind was on the flowers that had not bloomed. What had happened? Had the sorcery ended? Had the djinns flown off somewhere else? Had Kaakkasseri Khayaluddin Thangal become bored of reading my mind?'

'Krishna, what happened with the case of the qabar?' I asked. He brightened right away.

We won in the High Court, chechi.'

'What does that mean?'

'The day after my housewarming, they are going to lay the foundation for the auditorium.'

I was speechless.

'So then, the qabar?'

'Oh, there is no qabar of historical significance there,' he scoffed. 'It's just what they believed.'

'So, who is buried there?'

'Oh, it's no relative of Kaakkasseri. It was a Nair aristocrat, the first one in the area to convert to Islam. When he came back after converting to Islam, the nephews got together and buried him in a pit. And to anyone who asked, they said he had gone to Kashi. The man who had climbed the palm to tap toddy saw them digging the pit at dawn. And he told the people working in the paddy fields. And the Thangals' ancestor heard about it from them.'

'Which ancestor of the Thangals?'

'He was a Jonakan. He had come from Turkey on business. A Nair woman from this patriarch's family was captivated by his beauty and left her home for him. That caused a ruckus among the Nairs. But the raja took the side of the Turk. Around then is when the old patriarch came back, having converted to Islam.

The Turk's wife cried when she heard that her uncle had been smothered in a pit. The Turk spoke to the king, and then had the old man's body exhumed and gave it an Islamic-style funeral. And that is the qabar of contention.'

Was it sorcery? I felt the ground tremble. I lost my balance. Still, I tried to act natural and asked, 'So, the other party, the architect. Where is he?'

'Ayyo, chechi! That's a tragedy. He had gone off to renovate some historical monument. A pillar toppled and fell on his head.'

With a sigh, Krishnakumar continued: 'It's only been an hour since he was declared brain dead.'

It must have been the rainbows that broke when the sky fell down. They stabbed my eyes. I closed my eyes and opened them. The sun had been extinguished. All around, I could only see darkness. Not even a firefly was visible. Krishnakumar said goodbye and left. Roshi entered. I sat calmly under the ruins of the sky. The clouds kept crumbling and falling. The clouds that I and Advaith and Kaakkasseri Thangal had touched and caressed. Feathery clouds as white as the marble of the house called Bhavana. Some of the clouds were stained red from the blood of birds that had grazed them. Some were grimy after brushing against broken rainbows. Heavy objects hit my throat one after the other. The minarets in the sky, the dust of clouds, the embers of stars, the cracks in the sun, the shards of the moon. Then, past the silver trees and the golden leaves, past the butterflies with blue wings, past the birds with yellow wings, past the girls whose feet didn't touch the ground, past all of it—the smell of something crushed and bruised. I longed to see my mother. I hoped that at least one of my mother's thirty-two children would scratch and claw and dig me up from where I was buried.

I put my head down on the desk. Someone came in and kept something on the desk. I didn't have the strength to raise my head. Pain was tearing me apart, destroying me. I was afraid that in my underbelly two embryos were teaching each other the vanishing trick. Slowly, very slowly, the fragrance of Edward roses spread all around me. Even then, I didn't dare open my eyes. What if the illusion shattered when I opened my eyes?

For the first time, I felt a sense of completeness in someone's absence.